Published by Hachette Partworks Ltd.
ISBN: 978-1-908648-89-1
Date of Printing: November 2013
Printed in Malaysia by Tien Wah Press

THE

LION KING

Disney
hachette

It was a beautiful African morning in the Pride Lands. All the animals assembled at Pride Rock. They came on padding paws, pounding hooves and flapping wings. King Mufasa and Queen Sarabi welcomed them warmly.

Today was a very special day. Simba, the first-born cub of Mufasa and Sarabi, would join the great Circle of Life. Rafiki, the wise old baboon, held up the little lion cub for all to see.

One animal did not join the happy gathering – Mufasa's brother, Scar. Jealous Scar dreamed of being king himself and had a plan to get rid of Mufasa and his son.

Simba grew quickly. One day, Uncle Scar told him about an elephant's graveyard under the cliff, where only the bravest lions dared to venture.

Of course, Simba couldn't wait to go there! He invited his best friend, Nala, to come along. But how could they get away when Zazu the hornbill, advisor to the king, was always watching them?

Eventually they found their way to the graveyard. Elephant bones poked out of the ground. Suddenly, three mean hyenas started chasing them – but then the giant bones were rattled by a mighty ***ROAR***!

It was Mufasa, the Lion King. He sprang at the hyenas and scared them off. Zazu had warned him that the cubs were in trouble.

Mufasa was angry with Simba.

"Aw, Dad," the cub protested. "I was only trying to be brave, like you."

"A good king is wise as well as brave," sighed Mufasa. He pointed up at the starry sky. "The great kings of the past look down on us. They will always be there to guide you… and so will I."

Later, Scar met with the hungry hyenas. He had another plan that would help him become king.

Next day, Scar took Simba into a rocky canyon.

"Wait here," he ordered. "Your father has a surprise for you."

"Will I like it?" Simba asked.

"Oh, it's to die for," sneered his uncle.

Scar signalled to the hyenas, who chased a huge herd of wildebeests into the canyon. Simba felt the earth shake. He managed to climb a dead tree and call for help.

Just as Scar planned, Mufasa raced to Simba's rescue. He lifted his son to safety, but then fell under the tide of stomping hooves.

Scar watched as his brother tried to pull himself up the steep rocks.

"Help me!" Mufasa pleaded. Scar reached for the Lion King's paws. He leaned close and whispered... "Long live the king." Then he let his brother tumble into the stampede.

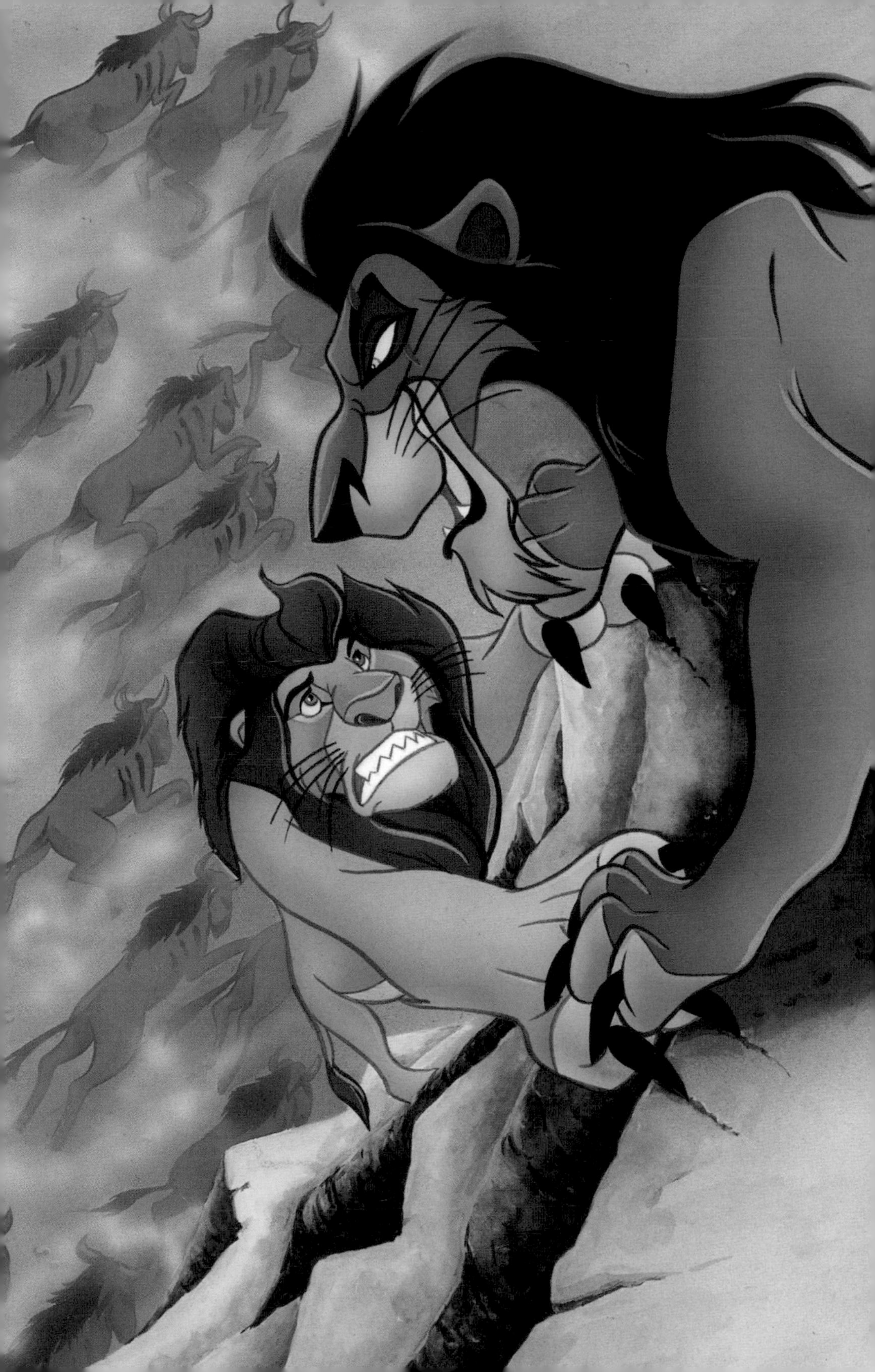

Simba found his father lying lifeless in the dust. "Nooooo!" he wailed.

Scar came to his side. "What have you done?"

"There were wildebeests... he tried to save me... I didn't mean to..." stammered Simba.

"If it weren't for you," said Scar, "he'd be alive."

Simba looked stricken. "What should I do?"

"Run away and never come back," advised Scar. Scar watched Simba run. Then he sent the hyenas after him.

Simba narrowly escaped the hyenas. Then he ran through the desert, not knowing where to go. Finally he collapsed, exhausted.

When he woke, he found he had two new companions – Timon the meerkat and Pumbaa the warthog. They fed him and gave him water.

Pumbaa and Timon taught Simba how to eat big, slimy grubs.

Soon, the three animals were the best of friends.

Many months passed. Gradually, Simba turned into a magnificent lion. One day, he heard his friends calling for help. They were being attacked by a hungry lioness! Simba fought her off, but then he recognised her – she was his childhood friend, Nala.

Nala told him that the Pride Lands were now ruled by Scar. All the animals were terrified of him.

"Come back and become king," she pleaded.

"I'm no king," growled Simba.

That night, Rafiki came to Simba. As they stood beneath the stars, Mufasa's face appeared.

"Simba," said Mufasa. "You have forgotten who you are and forgotten me. Look inside yourself. You must take your place in the Circle of Life!"

Simba knew his father was right. With his friends, he returned to the Pride Lands.

Back at Pride Rock, King Scar couldn't believe his eyes. "Mufasa? It can't be. You're dead!" But Sarabi recognised her son. "Simba!" she gasped.

Scar and the hyenas pushed Simba to the edge of the rock. "This is just the way your father looked before I killed him," snarled Scar. Now Simba knew the truth. He leapt at Scar, who tumbled into the mob of hungry hyenas.

Simba roared. He was king. And as his queen, he chose the beautiful Nala.

Soon, a new prince was presented at Pride Rock. All the animals gathered to see the first-born cub of King Simba and Queen Nala. And as Rafiki held up the cub, everyone knew that a future Lion King had joined the great Circle of Life.